D0606378

Brand-New Baby BLUES

WORDS BY
Kathi Appelt
ILLUSTRATIONS BY
Kelly Murphy

HARPER
An Imprint of HarperCollinsPublishers

Brand-New Baby Blues

Manufactured in China.

Library of Congress Cataloging-in-Publication Data
Appelt, Kathi.
Brand-new baby blues / words by Kathi Appelt ; illustrations by Kelly Murphy. — 1st ed.
p. cm.
Summary: The arrival of a new little brother has his big sister singing the blues.
ISBN 978-0-06-053233-8 (trade bdg.) — ISBN 978-0-06-053234-5 (lib bdg.)
[1. Stories in rhyme. 2. Babies—Fiction. 3. Brothers and sisters—Fiction.] I. Murphy, Kelly, ill. II. Title.
PZ8.3.A554Br 2010 2008005796
[E]-dc22 CIP
AC

Typography by Dana Fritts 10 11 12 13 SCP 10 9 8 7 6 5 4 3 2 ❖ First Edition

For Big Sister Bella and
Little Brother Maddox
—K.A.

For Madison, Logan, and
new (but not for long) baby Caden
—K.M.

Once upon a time
I was the only one,
I was the cat's pajamas,
I was the moon and sun.

It was me and only me—
I was the icing on the cake.
I was the royal pooh-bah,
the chocolate in the shake.

Now everything is different,
everything is changed.
I'm not the one and only.
My whole life's rearranged.

Those good ol' days are over.
It's official, it's the news!
With my brand-new baby brother
came the brand-new baby blues!

Once everything was peachy,
once everything was fine.
Now my brand-new baby brother
takes up all my mama's time.

“Not now” is all she answers
when I want to play a game.
It’s looking like my perfect life
will never be the same.

And you should see my daddy
make an oogly, googly face.
He never even looks at ME—
this brother took my place.

COLOR

It makes me sad, it makes me mad,
it makes me want to roar!
It makes me want to stomp my feet
across the kitchen floor.

'Cause the good ol' days are over.
It's official, it's the news!
With my brand-new baby brother
came the brand-new baby blues!

I liked it so much better then,
when it was only me.
Not a single baby anywhere.

It was . . .

heavenly.

There was no one in my mama's lap
when it was time to snuggle;

there was no one in my daddy's arms
when it was time to huggle.

Now he's wearing my old jammies,
he sleeps in my old bed,
he's got my favorite baby bear
beside his baby head.

All he does is sleep and eat.
There's not much he can do.
And when his diaper's dirty . . .
Yikes! It's yabba dabba pew!

And look at him, all wrinkled up.
He really is a mess . . .
his little nose, his little toes . . .
he's cute enough . . . I guess.

And even though he cries a lot
and causes lots of troubles,
I've never seen a baby blow
so many awesome bubbles!

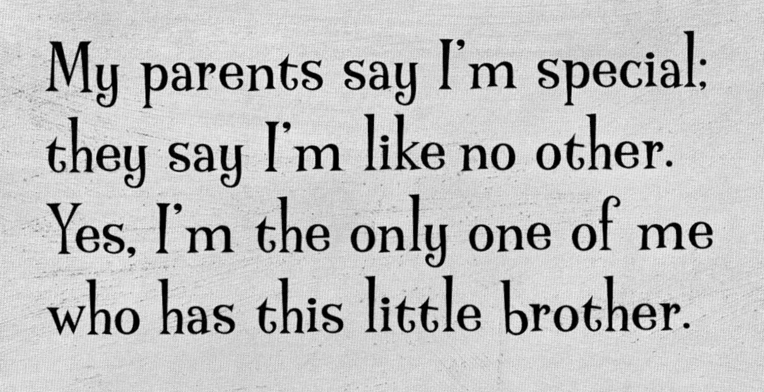

My parents say I'm special;
they say I'm like no other.
Yes, I'm the only one of me
who has this little brother.

So I guess he's really not all bad
in a baby sort of way.
Of course he'll be much better
when he's old enough to play.

Hide-and-seek will be a blast
when I'm not the only "it."
And I can hardly wait
to teach this baby how to spit.

We'll catch a ball and fly a kite . . .
it's looking like, just maybe,
he'll be a lot more fun
when he's a brother, not a baby!

Still, those good ol' days are over.
It's official, it's the news!
With my brand-new baby brother
came the brand-new baby blues!